TALLY CAT
KEEPS TRACK

BY Trudy Harris ILLUSTRATED BY Andrew N. Harris

M MILLBROOK PRESS / MINNEAPOLIS

Tally McNally was an alley cat
but more than that—A TALLY CAT.

3

TIMES RIGHT

STRIPES
IIII

BOOTS
IIII IIII

TALLY
IIII IIII IIII

He kept a tally all day long
of who was right and who was wrong,

of who was tall and who was taller,

of who was small and who was smaller.

And when all things were said and done,
Tally McNally always won.

He went

SCRATCH, SCRATCH, SCRITCHY,
SCRATCH, SCRATCH.

TIMES I WON
TODAY

One day, Tom Cat, splattered with rain,
plopped in a chair and began to complain,

"I'm soaked to my skin. No cat is as wet."

But Tally McNally said slyly, "Not yet . . ."

"Ten drops for you and sixteen for me
means I'm the wettest.
You'll have to agree."

WATER DROPS

TOM - ~~IIII~~ ~~IIII~~

TALLY - ~~IIII~~ ~~IIII~~ ~~IIII~~ I

Then he stood on a box
and announced with a grin,
"I'm Tally McNally,
and I always win."

SCRATCH, SCRATCH,
SCRITCHY,
SCRATCH, SCRATCH.

"No way!" shouted Tom Cat.
"I say you're a cheat!
To settle this fairly, let's meet in the street."

Tom dove in a puddle,
and rainwater rose
over his chin to the tip of his nose.
He jumped to his feet and declared,
"Now I'm wetter.
Admit it, McNally,
I'm wetter.
I'm better."

"Not true," replied Tally.
"The score is now tied.
You're the winner out here,
but *I* won inside."

So

SCRATCH, SCRATCH, SCRITCHY, SCRATCH, SCRATCH.

WETTEST
INSIDE
TOM TALLY
1

WETTEST
OUTSIDE
TOM TALLY
1

"I'll do even better,"
they heard Tally utter
as Tally McNally
slid down the gutter.

"Stop!" shouted Tom Cat.
Kitty yelled, "Wait!"

But sadly for Tally,
their calls came too late.

He went
SCRATCH, SCRATCH, SCRITCHY,
SCRATCH, . . . SPLASH!

"Help!" shouted Tally, "I'm stuck in the drain!
I don't want to be wetter. I'm sick of the rain."

"But how can we help you?
You're so deep below."

"Just run and find Boots.
She's the smartest. She'll know."

Boots stretched toward Tally, then said with a frown,
"I can't reach him either. He's much too far down.
We need someone taller, but who could that be?"
From below, a voice came, "Stripes is tallest. You'll see."

They went

SEARCH, SEARCH, SEARCHY,
SEARCH, SEARCH.

Stripes stretched, and he stretched
with all of his might.
But Tally McNally remained out of sight.

"If Stripes cannot get him, none of us can,"
Boots said. Then she added, "We need a new plan.
We don't just need taller. We also need smaller."

"Well, Kitty's the one," they heard Tally holler.

"We need smallest and tallest
and smartest, and yet,
we still need another
(who'll have to get wet)."

Boots whispered her plan
as they stood in a huddle.

Then one by one,
they all lay by the puddle.

Paw in paw, they formed a long chain
and lowered poor Tom
down the dark, dank drain.

STRETCH, STRETCH, STRITCHY,
STRETCH, STRETCH.

DAYS STUCK
IN THE DRAIN
1

"Hooray!" they all shouted. "We've finally got him."
And out of the hole, together, they brought him.

After high fives and hugs, they waved to McNally.
Then back in the alley, he made one last tally.

TALLY UP

Have you ever used your fingers to help you count? Using fingers is one way to keep track of the number of things we are counting. But sometimes, the items we are counting total more than our ten fingers.

Tallying is another way for people to keep track of things they count. Tally marks look like this:

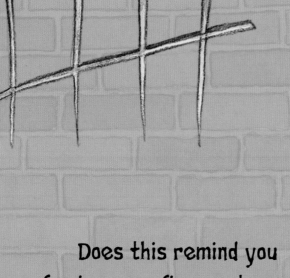

Does this remind you
of using your fingers to count?

To tally, we count "1, 2, 3, 4, tally cross 5." Each tally line represents one thing that we are counting. We can continue counting by adding more tally lines or marks: "6, 7, 8, 9, tally cross 10." The next group would be "11, 12, 13, 14, tally cross 15." When we count groups of tallies, we count by fives. For any leftover marks (groups less than five), we keep counting by ones. The numbers below end with a group of three: 16, 17, 18.

With tallying, we can keep track of more than one thing at a time. In our story, on page 5 Tally McNally kept track of his cans and Stripes's cans. Each time a can was added to Stripes's pile, Tally added one mark by Stripes's name. Each time a can was added to Tally's pile, he added a mark by his own name. This would have been a great way to see who was taller—if all the cans had been the same size. But that sneaky Tally scrunched some of his cans. That way he could add more cans to his tally and make it look like he was taller. Can you tell how he tried to trick Kitty on page 6 so that his tally was smaller?

To the Cranes and the Parrys, friends forever
—T.H.

For Kate, the cutest two-year-old in the world,
and Jack, Gus, and Spot, the best mice catchers in the West
—A.N.H.

Text copyright © 2011 by Trudy Harris
Illustrations copyright © 2011 by Andrew N. Harris

Millbrook Press
A division of Lerner Publishing Group, Inc.
241 First Avenue North
Minneapolis, MN 55401 U.S.A.

Website address: www.lernerbooks.com

Library of Congress Cataloging-in-Publication Data

Harris, Trudy.
    Tally cat keeps track / by Trudy Harris ; illustrated by Andrew N. Harris.
        p.   cm. — (Math is fun!)
    Summary: Alley cat Tally McNally loves to tally and loves to win, but when his competitive streak gets him into trouble, he has to rely on his friends for help.
    ISBN: 978-0-7613-4451-3 (lib. bdg. : alk. paper)
    [1. Stories in rhyme. 2. Counting—Fiction. 3. Cats—Fiction. 4. Friendship—Fiction. 5. Mathematics—Fiction.] I. Harris, Andrew, 1977– ill. II. Title.
    PZ8.3.H24318Tal 2010
    [E]—dc22   2009049586

Manufactured in the United States of America
1 – DP – 7/15/10